THE DARK REALM

STING
THE SCORPION
MAN

With special thanks to Lucy Courtenay

To Anna McCullough

www.beastquest.co.uk

ORCHARD BOOKS
338 Euston Road, London NW1 3BH
Orchard Books Australia
Level 17/207 Kent St, Sydney, NSW 2000

A Paperback Original
First published in Great Britain in 2008

Beast Quest is a registered trademark of Working Partners Limited
Series created by Working Partners Limited, London

Text © Working Partners Limited 2008
Cover illustration and inside illustrations by Steve Sims
© Orchard Books 2008

ISBN 978 1 40830 003 9

10

Printed in Great Britain by J F Print Ltd.,
Sparkford, Somerset

The paper and board used in this paperback are natural recyclable
products made from wood grown in sustainable forests. The
manufacturing processes conform to the environmental regulations
of the country of origin.

Orchard Books is a division of Hachette Children's Books,
an Hachette UK company.

www.hachette.co.uk

STinG
THE SCORPION
MAN

BY ADAM BLADE

ORCHARD BOOKS

WELL

CITY
GATES

MALVEL'S
CASTLE

THE WESTERN CITY

THE RIV

GATEWAY TO
AVANTIA

MARSHES

Welcome. You stand on the edge of darkness, at the gates of an awful land. This place is Gorgonia, the Dark Realm, where the sky is red, the water black and Malvel rules. Tom and Elenna – your hero and his companion – must travel here to complete the next Beast Quest.

Gorgonia is home to six of the deadliest Beasts imaginable – minotaur, winged stallion, sea monster, Gorgon hound, mighty mammoth and scorpion man. Nothing can prepare Tom and Elenna for what they are about to face. Their past victories mean nothing. Only strong hearts and determination will save them now.

Dare you follow Tom's path once more? I advise you to turn back. Heroes can be stubborn and adventures may beckon, but if you decide to stay with Tom, you must be brave and fearless. Anything less will mean certain doom.

Watch where you step...

Kerlo the Gatekeeper

PROLOGUE

The Gorgonian medicine woman twitched and muttered in her sleep. Her dreams were strange tonight.

A boy stood alone in a dark tunnel, his face bloody and streaked with sweat. In his hand was a battered wooden shield with six tokens embedded in its surface. Torches flickered along the long passageway, throwing the boy's shadow onto the wall, where it stood huge and alone.

The boy was suddenly dwarfed by a second silhouette – a Beast with a sweeping tail and monstrous pincers which snipped and slashed at the air.

A giant scorpion!

The medicine woman moaned in her sleep as the silhouette grew clearer. The creature was more than a scorpion. It was half-man!

The boy whirled around, raising his sword, as the Beast attacked with its razor-sharp pincers.

"Tom!"

A girl's voice screamed. It was Elenna, the girl the medicine woman had helped to heal. She stood with a wolf by her side and held a bow with an arrow in the bow-string. She let the arrow fly at the scorpion, but it bounced harmlessly off the creature's body. The boy stumbled and the Beast reared up, its pincers snapping viciously and slicing ever closer to the boy's head.

The medicine woman woke from her dream with a gasp. She sat upright, clutching her blankets, her heart hammering. A tiny scorpion lay at the bottom of her bed. She got up, her eyes never leaving the creature's

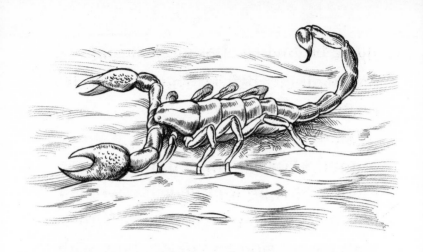

glossy black body. Her nightmare
had saved her life. Many Gorgonians
had been found dead in their beds
because a poisonous scorpion had
found its way under the covers.

She pushed her way out of the
tent. The boy's face was still clear in
her mind. Tom. She had heard that
name recently. Elenna had
mentioned it. Tom was her friend.

Shivering, the old woman tried to
shake off the feeling of dread that
had crept over her. The dream was a

sign of things to come. She'd had premonitions before. She hoped this one was wrong.

"Stay safe, Elenna and Tom," she muttered, gazing up at the swirling red sky of Gorgonia.

Scorpions were bad enough.

A giant scorpion would be unstoppable.

CHAPTER ONE

DESTINY IN THE WEST

The blood-red light from the
Gorgonian sunrise peeped through
the trees as Tom and Elenna made
their way out of the forest, their
faithful companions, Storm and
Silver, ambling beside them.
Vulture-like birds croaked on the
branches overhead, and a thick mist
lay on the ground.

Tom led the way, holding Storm's bridle. He noticed that Elenna kept her hand protectively on one of Silver's shaggy shoulders. The wolf had been badly wounded two Quests previously, and had only just returned to Elenna's side. Tom and his friends had already freed five of Avantia's Beasts from Malvel's kingdom. Arcta the mountain giant was the last of the six Beasts being kept here against his will by the evil wizard. If they could free Arcta, their Quest would be complete.

Tom pulled his shield from his shoulder and studied the tokens set into its scarred wooden surface. Gifts from the good Beasts, they usually glowed and vibrated when a Beast was in danger. But Arcta's eagle feather remained dark, and the shield had been still for far too long. Where was Malvel keeping the mountain giant?

"Still nothing?" Elenna asked.

Tom shook his head. "It's as if Arcta is somewhere so far away that the shield can't sense him." He pushed his shield over his shoulder again, refusing to meet Elenna's eyes. He didn't want to reveal his worst fear: that Arcta was already dead. "Perhaps the map will give us some clues," he said instead.

He took the smelly, worn parchment from Storm's saddlebag. Malvel had given them the map when they first entered Gorgonia. Each time they began searching for a good Beast the map would give Tom a sign that he could use, or a green line would snake across its surface for Tom and Elenna to follow. Usually these signs and pathways would lead to trouble, but it was the only map that Tom and Elenna had.

"Nothing," Tom said, looking down at the map in disappointment.

"We can't trust it anyway," Elenna pointed out as Tom put the map away.

"You're right," Tom replied. "I'll use my compass instead. It won't let us down."

Tom's uncle had given him the silver compass on his first birthday as a hero. Instead of north, south, east and west, the words *Destiny* and *Danger* were inscribed upon its face. The compass had belonged to his father, Taladon, who was once the Master of the Beasts for Avantia and had disappeared when Tom was a baby.

Tom held the compass and walked in a complete circle. As he pointed it to the west, the arrow whirled several times and came to rest on *Destiny*.

Tom felt his heart lift. He put the compass away. "The compass is telling us to go west," he said to Elenna. "I'm sure that's where Arcta is. While there's blood in my veins, I will find him and get him home to Avantia!"

Storm neighed and tossed his black mane as if he were agreeing. Silver sprang ahead down the path, eager to get going, and Tom and Elenna pressed on after him.

In the far distance, they saw something lying on the ground.

"What's that?" Elenna asked, shading her eyes in the red light.

Tom used the power of the magical golden helmet to bring the object into focus. Although the precious golden armour had been returned to Avantia at the end of the last Quest, he still possessed its gifts, and the helmet gave him extra-keen vision.

It was a boy, sprawled on the ground and riddled with arrows. His body was twitching. Tom felt his skin turn cold.

"It's Seth," he said to Elenna. "He's hurt."

Seth was one of Malvel's servants. Tom and Elenna had fought him before, and the boy had been intent on killing them.

"Do we help?" Elenna asked.

Tom hesitated.

Seth was his sworn enemy. What should he do?

CHAPTER TWO

DARK SURPRISE

Seth suddenly let out a groan of agony that echoed through the trees.

Tom knew what he had to do. He couldn't ignore another person in pain, even if that person was his enemy. To do such a thing would make him as bad as Malvel.

Tom tugged Storm's bridle, leading the black stallion towards the figure. Elenna walked next to him, with

Silver pressed close to her side.

The path broadened and the trees thinned out to reveal a black, mirror-like lake. Seth lay close to the water's edge. He was still breathing, but only just. His ribcage rose and fell in shallow gasps. Six arrows were embedded in his chest, and his blood had seeped onto the ground. It seemed impossible that he was still alive.

Tom was now close enough to see the beads of sweat on Seth's forehead. Storm dug his hooves into the path then stepped backwards. His nostrils flared.

"Hush, Storm," Tom said, soothing his horse.

"Silver doesn't like this, either, Tom." Elenna gazed down at her wolf. Silver's growls were deepening, and the hair on his back was standing up.

"Seth can't do anything to us," Tom reasoned. "Look at him. He needs our help."

He gave Storm's bridle to Elenna. Then he took hold of Epos the flame bird's talon and pulled it from the front of his shield, before kneeling down next to Seth. As gently as he could, he pulled three arrows out of the boy's body and held the phoenix's talon to each wound. Seth's skin instantly began to knit together, and one by one the wounds started to heal.

Seth's groaning eased. His eyes fluttered open. Seeing Tom, he cried out in panic. "No! Leave me alone!"

Ignoring Seth, Tom pulled the fourth arrow from the boy's chest and healed the gaping hole.

Seth's eyes filled with terror. He began pushing Tom away, as his strength started to return. "You don't know what you're doing!" he gasped. "You should have left me to die!"

Tom ignored him. He took hold of the fifth arrow and pulled.

With surprising speed, Seth grabbed Tom's wrist and pushed the arrow back into himself with a scream of pain. Tom heard Elenna gasp with horror.

Storm whinnied and tried
to pull away from Elenna's grasp,
while Silver stood still, his tail
between his legs.

Tom could understand why his
friends were so spooked. It was as if
Seth wanted to die.

He steadied his hands and swiftly
prised Seth's fingers away from the
arrow, drawing the dripping shaft out
of the boy's flesh.

"No," Seth moaned, as Tom took
hold of the sixth and final arrow.
"Don't do it."

"Something is wrong here, Tom,"
Elenna said, shaking her head.
"I think we should respect Seth's
wishes and leave him."

"He's mad with pain," Tom
reassured his friend. "There's just one
more arrow…"

Tom pulled the sixth arrow loose. Seth lashed out with his fists as Tom held the phoenix talon to the fifth and sixth wounds, but he was too weak to knock Tom's hands away. In an instant, the wounds had healed.

Seth let out an unearthly screech and writhed on the ground, making Tom jump back in alarm. Elenna desperately attempted to soothe Storm and Silver as they tried to turn tail and run.

Something was happening to Seth. Something awful...

They watched in horror as the boy's legs fused together, forming a single limb that lengthened and tore through his clothes. It grew darker and harder until it turned into a bulbous, beaded tail. The tail swiped out powerfully at Tom and Elenna,

knocking them both to the ground.

Seth screamed again. His voice sounded deeper and rougher. Three legs forced their way out of both sides of his torso, tearing through his tunic.

"Get back!" Tom shouted to Elenna as they both scrambled to their feet.

Seth sprang onto his new legs and let out a horrifying roar as his arms stiffened and distorted into two pincers. They began clicking and snapping in Tom and Elenna's direction. Tom could hardly believe what was in front of him. The bottom part of Seth's body looked just like a scorpion, but his chest and head were still human. Seth pointed at Tom and Elenna, his face a mask of anger and despair.

"You!" he screamed, his voice terrifyingly deep. "This is your fault! This is Malvel's punishment for my failure. If you'd just let me die as I wished, this wouldn't have happened. I wouldn't be a monster!"

With a roar of fury, Seth picked up his sword, which had been lying by the side of the path. Its wickedly

serrated edge glinted in the blood-red
light. With his giant scorpion pincers
snapping, he advanced on Tom and
Elenna.

CHAPTER THREE

THE BATTLE BY THE LAKE

"Don't come any closer," Tom ordered, pointing his blade at the creature in front of him.

Seth gave a ghastly chuckle. His long tail reared high in the air, ready to strike.

"Tom," Elenna gasped, staring up. "Look!"

Tom followed her gaze. Something

was gleaming at the tip of Seth's tail – a purple jewel. Instinctively, Tom touched the belt he wore around his waist – a belt already decorated with five jewels, each taken from the Beasts of Gorgonia… If Seth had a jewel, it could only mean one thing.

"Seth's an evil Beast now," Tom whispered to Elenna. "The last one we must defeat."

"Enough talking!" Seth roared, lunging at them.

Elenna dived away, while Tom dodged to one side. He found himself next to the black lake that lay beside the path, and heard a rush of air as Elenna released her arrow. But the shaft bounced harmlessly off Seth's scaly tail.

Seth swung his sword above his head and sprang towards Tom. He moved so fast that Tom had to use the magical power of the golden boots to leap into the air and avoid the vicious blade. The tip of Seth's sword missed Tom's stomach by a whisker.

The momentum of Seth's attack carried him to the edge of the lake, where he teetered for a moment on the bank, desperately struggling to stay upright. Then he looked down at his reflection in the black water and Tom saw his face sag in horror.

"I'm hideous!" Seth screamed in despair, falling to the ground, away from his reflection.

Tom felt a surge of pity for the vile creature in front of him, but there were no words that could possibly offer comfort. Tom turned and joined Elenna, who was standing with

Storm and Silver. As he did so, a
swirling red cloud dropped out of
the sky and surrounded them. A tall
wizard in blood-red robes stepped
out of the scarlet mist.

"Malvel!" Tom gasped.

The Dark Wizard inclined his head.
"The young hero," he said, a thin
smile spreading across his face.
"I knew your good heart would get
you into trouble one day."

Tom realised now that this was all
part of Malvel's plan. The wizard
knew he would try to help the
injured Seth. Angrily, Tom levelled his
sword at him, ready to do battle. But
with a wave of one thin hand, Malvel
placed a shimmering magical barrier
in front of himself and Seth. Growling
furiously, Silver hurled himself at
the barrier, but he bounced off the
magical shield with a yelp, almost as
if he had been burnt by fire.

"I beg you, Malvel," Seth sobbed,
collapsing before the wizard. "Turn
me back to how I was!"

Tom saw the wizard look coldly at

his servant. "Stop snivelling," Malvel commanded. "This is your punishment for failing me so many times. You are no longer Seth, but shall be called Sting the scorpion man. And I command you, Beast, to go to the Western City of Gorgonia and guard Arcta the mountain giant."

Sting bowed his head in defeat.

Malvel conjured a shining red orb from the air, which pulsed and grew in his hand, then he threw it at Sting, imprisoning the new Beast in its blood-red heart.

Muttering in a language that Tom didn't understand, Malvel clapped his hands together three times. The giant red orb rose into the air and, with a flick of his long, bony finger, Malvel sent it west, towards the mountains. In an instant, the orb was out of sight.

The Western City. Tom gazed at the mountains on the horizon, committing them to his magical super-memory, a power he had won when he defeated Narga the sea monster. The orb may have flown too fast for him to follow its exact path, but Tom felt sure that the

Western City lay somewhere in those mountains.

He was torn from his thoughts by Malvel's cruel and cackling laughter.

"I know what you are planning," sneered the evil wizard. "But don't bother to follow Sting. There is no way that you will ever find Arcta."

With a final screech of laughter, Malvel wrapped himself in red mist and disappeared.

"He's wrong," Tom told Elenna fiercely, pulling himself into Storm's saddle. "We will find Arcta and we will get him home."

Elenna nodded, looking as determined as Tom felt. Silver nosed around her feet as she picked up the arrow she had fired at Sting. She then slung her bow over her shoulder and climbed into the saddle.

Tom gazed to the west, where two Beasts – one good and one bad – awaited them. "We're coming, Arcta," he whispered. "And we will never stop looking for you. Not while there's blood in our veins."

CHAPTER FOUR

THE VOICE IN THE WELL

The forest path wound along the shore of the black lake, emerging onto a wide open plain that ended at the line of black mountains where the red orb had disappeared.

Grabbing Malvel's map, Tom found the Western City. But the map was playing a new trick, one that Tom had never seen before. The image of the Western City floated across the ragged parchment, shifting mischievously from one place to the next.

"The map is no good to us," Tom said. "All we can do is head through the mountains and hope to find the Western City for ourselves."

Elenna nodded, and they pushed forwards.

Gradually the terrain grew rougher and the track narrowed as they approached the mountains. Tom rode Storm carefully, avoiding any sharp stones that might lame the stallion. Soon the path disappeared completely, and they had to weave through stunted black shrubs and trees, whose twigs and branches caught at their clothes and whipped cruelly across their skin. The blood-red sun climbed higher, and the air was searing hot.

After half a day of moving through the arid heat, they found themselves back on a stony path, and Tom spotted a cluster of dull red towers in a cleft between two mountains. He took out Malvel's map and looked at the image of the Western City, which flitted across the parchment like a ghost. Its walls were red, just like the towers he could see ahead.

"I think we've found the Western City," Tom said eagerly, reining in Storm so that the stallion could rest.

Elenna and Silver both sat down on the hot, dry ground. As Tom replaced the map in the saddlebag, he felt Storm's heaving sides. The stallion was panting heavily in the heat. Looking around, Tom saw a well a little further on.

He pointed it out to Elenna. "Let's get some water," he suggested, and guided Storm towards the well. Elenna and Silver followed close behind.

They leant over the circular wall of the well and peered inside, hoping to see a long dark shaft and the welcome glint of water at the bottom. But there was nothing but a pile of rubble and loose stones. The sides of the well had collapsed inwards, blocking it up completely.

Tom rested his head on Storm's sweaty flank. "I'm sorry, boy," he said. "We'll find some water soon, I promise."

Storm whinnied trustingly and pushed at Tom's shoulder with his velvety black nose.

"Perhaps there will be another well closer to the city gates," Elenna said, shading her eyes from the glare of the sun as she stared up at the Western City. They were now a little closer, and the dark red walls gleamed in the sunlight.

"Hmm, I'm not sure that there are any more arou—" Tom broke off as the earth suddenly rumbled beneath their feet. Storm reared up, and Silver growled and retreated behind Elenna's legs.

"What was that?" Elenna said nervously. "An earthquake?"

Tom felt a tingling sensation rush up his arm from his shield. Arcta's token was vibrating! The earth rumbled again. The movement seemed to be coming from the broken well. Tom leant over the lip of the well and listened. The rumbling was an echoing roar. Tom recognised it immediately.

"It's Arcta!" he cried.

The giant roared again. The ground shook once more.

"What is he saying?" Elenna asked.

Thanks to the red jewel set into his belt, Tom could understand the good Beasts of Avantia as never before. Now, he sensed the giant's rage. "He's angry," he said, trying to explain the feelings that were running through him as he listened to Arcta. "He's trapped somewhere underneath the Western City. He can't breathe properly – he feels like he's choking."

"We have to get underground straightaway and help him," Elenna said determinedly.

"Maybe we can climb down the well shaft and look for some kind of underground channel that will take us into the city," Tom suggested.

Elenna nodded. "You'll have to move some of these rocks," she said.

"I'll help as much as I can."

The golden breastplate had given Tom the gift of great strength. He seized the boulders that blocked the mouth of the well and heaved them aside as if they were feather pillows. Elenna took care of some of the smaller rocks. Before long, they had cleared a dark space in the well shaft. But the old walls of the well had relied for too long on the support of the boulders, and now they collapsed. They could no longer hear Arcta's voice.

"It's no good," Tom said.

"We'll have to head into the Western City." Elenna said thoughtfully. "I'm sure we'll be able to find a way underground once we're there."

"True," Tom said. "If a giant the size of five men can be taken underground inside the Western City, then there'll be a very big trap door somewhere, right?"

"Right!" Elenna agreed.

Together, the four companions moved along the scrub-covered track that led to the gates of the Western City.

Tom hoped he was right about the trap door. They didn't have much time – and Arcta's life was hanging in the balance…

CHAPTER FIVE

THE GATEKEEPER

As they approached the gates, Tom felt all his senses sharpening. He glanced around. From the moment he and Elenna had arrived in Gorgonia, Malvel had put a price on their heads. Who knew how many bounty hunters were waiting among the rocks ready to capture or kill them? The closer they got to the city, the greater the danger became.

They won't catch us, Tom thought fiercely. *We'll fight to the death if we have to!*

The great red city loomed up in front of them. Its defensive walls towered overhead and were streaked with slime. Skulls were set into the brickwork and evil-looking spikes lined the top of the walls, their tips glinting in the red sun. The city's huge black gates were firmly closed. But there was no sign of any guards.

Silver growled uncertainly as Tom and Elenna stopped in front of the silent gates, and Storm pawed the ground anxiously.

Tom dismounted and gazed around. "Why are there no guards?" he asked Elenna.

"Perhaps it's a trap," Elenna replied uneasily.

There was a sudden movement from behind one of the trees that flanked the gates. A thin man in old brown robes, wearing a tattered eyepatch and holding a walking stick, stepped out to stand before them.

Tom recognised him at once. "Kerlo!" he said.

"Hello," Kerlo replied. "If you wish it, I will let you into the city."

Tom wasn't sure that he trusted Kerlo, even though the Gorgonian gatekeeper had helped them more than once. Instinctively, his hand went to his sword. Elenna, too, held her bow and arrow at the ready.

Kerlo shook his head sadly. "Still so suspicious," he muttered. "Have I not been an ally on your Quest? Have I not aided you?"

"But why do you help us?" Tom challenged. "What's in it for you?"

Kerlo rested his weight on the long wooden stick that he held in his gnarled hands. "I was once a good wizard," he said quietly. "I tried to help the rebels in their fight against Malvel, but the Dark Wizard's magic was more powerful than I had ever imagined. He condemned me to spend an eternity as gatekeeper – between worlds." His face grew bleak. "I have not been able to cross a threshold in many years. I cannot even enter my family home." The gatekeeper fell silent for a moment. "You must understand, home is like a jewel and it is only once it has gone that you realise how precious it is."

"We thank you for all you have done, Kerlo," Elenna said. "Will you help us get into the Western City?"

Kerlo nodded. "Once inside, you must head to Malvel's castle," he said. "In the castle's courtyard, you will find a trap door which leads to the cemetery that lies beneath the city. Those catacombs might be just the place to hide a giant Beast."

Kerlo held his hands out towards the gates. With a crash that shook the ground, the huge iron doors swung open. As they walked through them, Tom saw that the entrance to the city

was set out as a series of three paths, just like the beginning of a maze. There were three possible routes into the city, but how could they be sure that they would choose the right one? And what would happen if they were wrong?

CHAPTER SIX

DANGER IN THE WESTERN CITY

Tom turned to ask Kerlo for advice. But the iron gates had already silently swung shut behind them and the gatekeeper was gone.

Tom thought quickly, then pulled out his silver compass. He aimed it at the path on their right. At once, the arrow swung to *Danger*. Tom moved the compass until it pointed at the central path. The needle flew to *Danger* again, quivering slightly this time. Then Tom turned the compass to the last of the three paths.

For what seemed an age, the needle hovered uncertainly. Tom was about to put the compass back into his pocket when the needle swung slowly around to *Destiny* and held steady.

"This way," said Tom, tugging at Storm's bridle.

They moved cautiously down the path. Blood-red walls flanked them on both sides. Overhead, the red sun hid behind black clouds, casting long, bruise-coloured shadows that seemed to bode ill. An archway loomed up ahead. Two Gorgonian guards were patrolling it, their weapons slung casually over their shoulders. Beyond the guards, Tom and Elenna could see a city square surging with strange-looking people, whose bodies seemed to be hunched and crooked.

"I think we need to try the direct approach," Tom whispered.

Elenna nodded.

"Hail!" Tom called out, taking Storm with him as he strode towards the guards.

"Who goes there?" called the first guard in a harsh, croaking voice.

"Two travellers," Elenna replied, coming to stand at Tom's side. Silver bounded up next to her.

The second guard narrowed his eyes. His gaze flicked to Storm and Silver, then back again. "What is your business in the Western City?" he growled.

"Rest," Tom replied, holding firmly

onto Storm's bridle. "Food. Will you let us pass?"

The first guard looked as if he were about to step aside. But then the second guard jabbed his finger in Elenna's direction. His eyes were suddenly full of greed. "I know you," he said. "You're wanted by Malvel. Your faces are on posters all over this city!"

The game was up. Using the power from his golden boots, Tom leapt and seized the guards around their thick necks, bringing their heads together with a loud *thunk*. The guards slumped to the ground, unconscious.

"Take their cloaks," Elenna said, looking all around her. "We can disguise our faces with the hoods."

Quickly they stripped off the guards' cloaks and flung them over themselves. After adjusting their hoods to make sure that no one could see their faces, they walked through the archway with Storm and Silver at their sides.

The city square was bustling with beings that didn't quite look human. Their eyes were yellow and their hair grew in ragged patches. Scarred, spotty skin hung loosely from their faces, and their teeth were black and pointed. With a shudder, Tom noticed that their hands looked like claws.

Keeping their heads down and holding tightly onto Storm and Silver, Tom and Elenna walked across the glossy black flagstones of the square.

Malvel's castle was impossible to miss. They could see it in the distance, on the fringes of the city. Forks of black lightning like huge lizard tongues flickered in the red sky above the castle's turrets, and Tom knew at once that it was the centre of all evil in Gorgonia.

The only way to reach the castle was to pass right through the centre of the city. Tom hoped that their disguises would hold out that long. He could see several "WANTED ALIVE" posters displaying their faces, stuck here and there on the city's slimy walls.

"There isn't much trade or bartering going on, is there?" Elenna whispered, glancing from left to right as they hurried on.

Tom nodded. It looked as if the

citizens of the Western City were more inclined to fight and argue than trade. Noisy skirmishes were breaking out all across the square.

A fight exploded between two men just as Tom and Elenna were passing.

"Give me my money!" screamed a ragged-looking fur-trader. "These are pure fox pelts!"

"Fox pelts?" his opponent roared back. "Cats, more like. You won't get any money from me!"

There was suddenly a whirl of fists and kicking legs, which Tom and Elenna managed to sidestep. Silver was not so lucky. The wolf gave a high-pitched yelp of pain as the fur-trader's heavy-soled boot caught him in the ribs.

"Silver!" Elenna gasped.

Without thinking, she ran to her

wolf's side and knelt down beside
him. As she did so, her hood fell back,
revealing her face.

There was a deathly hush in the
square, followed by shouts of
recognition.

"Avantians!"

"Elenna!" Tom shouted, his own
hood falling away from his face.
"They know it's us! Run!"

CHAPTER SEVEN

MALVEL'S CASTLE

Hordes of Gorgonians lunged towards
Tom and Elenna, their scaly arms
outstretched and their fists swinging.
With his super-strength, Tom threw
off the approaching attackers as easily
as if they were ragdolls.

Barrelling through the angry mob
he cleared a path across the square.
Elenna leapt nimbly onto Storm's
back, and the horse lashed out with

his hard hooves as the Gorgonians tried to close in again. Elenna galloped after Tom, with Silver nipping fiercely at the ankles of any Gorgonian foolish enough to get in their way.

Tom grabbed his sword and flashed it left and right in warning. Elenna then galloped close enough for him to seize a handful of Storm's mane and pull himself into the saddle. They broke free of the attackers and raced towards the castle. Storm's black tail rippled out like silk, and Silver was a blur of grey fur as he sprinted at their side.

As they approached the castle, Tom used his super-sight to check how many guards were on the gates. He didn't like what he saw. Two armed guards were on patrol.

Various weapons hung from their waists, and they each held a wicked-looking sword.

Keeping out of sight of the guards, Elenna turned Storm's head and they raced into a copse of trees at the foot of the castle walls.

"We'll never get past them," Tom said, dismounting. "I'll send my shadow in to find an alternative route."

"Good idea," said Elenna, jumping from Storm's back.

The white jewel that Tom had won when he defeated Kaymon the Gorgon hound had given him the gift of being able to send his shadow away from himself. However, Tom could not move while he and his shadow were separated. Tom and Elenna settled themselves on a rock which gave a good view of the castle.

"Go, shadow," he ordered. "Find a way inside Malvel's castle."

The shadow peeled itself away from him, slipping over rocks and between trees, until it could press itself up against the castle walls. The guards noticed nothing. It glided along the stone, feeling for any nooks and possible entrances with its thin black fingers.

"Anything?" Elenna whispered to Tom.

"Nothing yet," Tom said, standing absolutely still.

The guards' voices carried to where Tom's shadow was standing. Through his shadow's ears, Tom could hear that they were arguing.

"I'm leaving," one of the guards was saying. "You do what you want."

"But—"

"Our shift's over," said the first guard impatiently. "So what if the next guards haven't arrived?"

"We're supposed to wait till they get here..."

The first guard snorted. "Wait all you like. I've got better things to do."

Hardly able to believe his luck, Tom watched through the eyes of his shadow as the first guard set off down the hill towards the city. After a moment's hesitation, the second guard followed. The gateway was clear.

Tom swiftly pulled his shadow back to him.

"Now's our chance," he told Elenna, jumping up into Storm's saddle. He held out his hand and helped his friend up behind him. "Quick, before the replacements get here."

Storm burst out from the cover of the trees and galloped through the unattended gate into the castle's courtyard, with Silver just behind.

Tom and Elenna leapt off the stallion and gazed around in awe. Malvel's castle was built entirely with polished black stone, streaked with gleaming stripes of red that pulsed like veins.

The trap door Kerlo had described was difficult to miss. It was so big it took up more than half of the courtyard.

"Just the right size for a giant," said Elenna grimly.

"Malvel must have taken Arcta down here," said Tom, walking over to where a huge iron ring was set into the trap door. "There's no other way he could have got him below the ground."

Storm whinnied and Tom glanced up at him. "We'll have to take Storm and Silver with us," he decided. "It's too risky to leave them behind. The replacement guards will be here soon."

Kneeling down, Tom took the huge iron ring in his hands. He braced himself, and pulled.

Thanks to the great strength given to him by the golden breastplate, he was able to turn it easily and the trap door opened with a gentle creak. A gigantic hole was revealed beneath it. Damp stone steps led down into darkness.

Tom lifted the huge door to shoulder-height and rested for a moment. It was taking all of his strength just to hold it.

"I'm going to have to push the door

right up and let it fall open," he said to Elenna. "Keep Storm and Silver out of the way."

"Won't that make too much noise?" Elenna asked, urging Storm and Silver to move back. "The guards will come running."

"We have no choice," Tom replied as he heaved the door upwards. "We've got to get down there and find Arcta."

He pushed the trap door all the way up, then let it fall backwards to the ground with a thundering crash.

Tom could hear shouts of alarm from deep inside the castle. "Follow the steps down!" he yelled to Elenna, grabbing Storm's bridle. "The guards are coming!"

CHAPTER EIGHT
THE TOMBS

They raced down the steps into the
yawning blackness of the tunnel.
Tom yanked hard at the two long
loops of rope that hung on the inner
side of the trap door. Creaking and
groaning, the door heaved slowly
upwards and then came crashing
down into place. Tom, Elenna and
their companions crouched in the
gloom and listened as guards ran into

the courtyard above them. Their muffled voices drifted down through the trap door.

"What was that noise?" one said. "For a moment, I thought the master's castle was crashing down about our ears."

"Sounded like the trap door," grunted another.

Tom held his breath. What if the guards worked out that there were intruders underground?

A third guard scoffed. "The only way to open that door is with a team of men and some of the master's most powerful horses. It'll be the giant, no doubt, kicking and screaming below ground."

Tom felt Elenna tense beside him at the mention of Arcta.

"He'll not be bothering us for much

longer," said a fourth voice. "Come on – we need to find out what that noise was. Let's check the outer walls of the castle; maybe something has collapsed there."

Tom listened to the retreating footsteps as the guards left the courtyard.

"What did they mean about Arcta?" Elenna asked once everything was silent.

"I don't know, but time is running out," said Tom. "We need to move."

He looked around at the tunnel. There appeared to be only one path leading away from the trap door and it was lit by flaming torches. The walls were rough, and pools of water lay in puddles on the ground.

Tom, Elenna and their animal companions raced through the

twisting passageway, which sank deeper into the ground with every turn. The sides of the tunnel grew smoother as they ran on, and Tom noticed with a chill the tombs that had been set into the tunnel walls. He remembered Kerlo's words. These were the catacombs: the place where the Gorgonians of the Western City buried their dead.

As he ran along, he couldn't help but read the names on the tombs by the flickering torchlight: Memnon, Arantis, Crestar, Xeropes...

Taladon.

Tom stopped dead at the smooth black tomb bearing his father's name. His breath caught in his throat. Taladon wasn't dead. He was Malvel's prisoner. Wasn't he?

"Tom?" Elenna turned and came

back up the tunnel to where he
was staring at the black tomb. She
held Storm's bridle tightly in one
hand and Silver loped behind her,
his eyes gleaming in the torchlight.
"What's wrong?"

"I have to open this tomb, Elenna,"
Tom said fiercely, drawing his sword.

"There's no time, Tom," Elenna
said. She seized his sleeve. "We have
to save Arcta."

Tom shook off Elenna's hand. His father might be lying here, right in front of him! He took a step back and smashed the butt of his sword into the face of the tomb. The stone cracked. Tom slammed his sword into the tomb several more times until it buckled, revealing a gaping black hole. But there was nothing inside. The tomb had never been used.

Elenna grabbed Tom's arm. "We have to hurry!"

Tom was about to reply when the red jewel on his belt began to glow and his head was suddenly filled with Arcta's voice. The good Beast was telling him once more that he was finding it hard to breathe. Tom whirled round and stared down the tunnel. He suddenly understood. Arcta had been buried alive in one of these tombs!

Tom was filled with remorse. Why
had he stopped to open Taladon's
tomb? It had been a selfish thing to
do and now Arcta's life was truly in
danger. Tom knew that he would
never forgive himself if they were
too late!

"Arcta is in real trouble," he said to
Elenna. "I've got to go."

"Hurry then; we'll catch up,"
Elenna replied.

Tom raced down the tunnel, using
the speed given to him by the golden
leg armour, and left his friends far
behind. The walls blurred around him
– and the tunnel suddenly opened up.
Tom skidded to a halt. He was in an
underground chamber with a low
roof. A massive tomb like a great
stone mountain stood in the centre of

the room. A name had been carved in huge letters on the tomb's side.

Arcta.

Tom's head pounded. He could sense that Arcta was weakening. There wasn't a moment to lose. He pulled his sword from its sheath and smashed it repeatedly into the side of the tomb. The echo of steel against stone boomed around the chamber. But the stone of this tomb was much thicker than that of Taladon's, and even with his huge strength, Tom couldn't break the tomb open.

Then he spotted a ledge, just above the tomb. If he could just get onto it, he could then try to lever the tomb open with his sword. Tom thought rapidly. The golden boots gave him the power to leap to great heights. He bunched his legs beneath him and jumped into the air, kicking off the giant tomb for an extra surge of height. With a thump, he landed on the stone ledge above the tomb. He then drew his sword and desperately started to lever up the lid.

Very slowly, it began to give. Tom worked hard, sweat pouring from his brow as he focused every drop of his magical strength on opening the tomb. At last, there was a gap wide enough for him to see into it.

Arcta lay very still, as if he were unconscious. His one great eye was closed. He was breathing in short, shallow gasps. Tom could see that he was bound by two huge silver chains that crossed over and around his vast, shaggy body.

With one more massive push, Tom shifted the lid off the tomb and stood

on the side of the casket. He raised
his sword above his head and brought
it down on one of the chains that
held Arcta. But the blade bounced
harmlessly away, the impact sending
fierce vibrations up Tom's arms. He
tried again and again, but he soon
realised that the chains were
enchanted and would not break. Tom
could feel despair threatening to
overwhelm him. How was he going
to free Arcta?

The sound of cantering hooves
echoed down the tunnel, and Storm,
Elenna and Silver raced into the
chamber.

"I can't do it, Elenna!" Tom panted,
shaking his head. "My sword isn't
strong enough to break the chains!"

"Don't lose hope, Tom!" Elenna
shouted up to him. "Remember the

gift of the golden chainmail? Strength of heart! You must believe in yourself. You must believe that you can do it!"

Tom lifted his sword shakily above his head. Closing his eyes, he concentrated with all his might. He could feel the magic of the golden armour pulsing in him. Bringing the sword down with a yell, Tom cut clean through one of the chains, which slithered away from Arcta's body like a silver snake. The mountain giant's eye fluttered open.

"One more blow, and you'll be free," Tom promised, and raised his sword for the second time.

But before Tom could bring his blade down, a hideous, jet-black tail came crashing through the chamber's wall...

Sting!

CHAPTER NINE

TRAPPED!

Tom gripped his sword tightly, ready
to fight, as the rest of the scorpion
man's body smashed through the
wall. How could he have forgotten?
Malvel had sent Sting to guard Arcta.
There was no way that he would let
Tom free the mountain giant without
a fight.

Fixing his gaze on Tom, Sting
scuttled across the chamber towards

him. He raised his pincers and clashed them together, the ghastly sound echoing around the rough stone walls.

"At last," Sting said in a voice that no longer held any trace of the boy Seth. "I will have revenge for all that you have cost me."

Tom knew he had to find some extra strength to fight Malvel's last Beast. Everything depended on it.

He sprang from the edge of the tomb and tumbled through the air, landing squarely on Sting's back. With a roar, the Beast thrashed his tail, and the purple jewel at the end of it just missed Tom's eye.

With lightning speed, Sting spun around. Caught off balance, Tom fell to the ground. He pulled his shield from his back and flung it over his head as a giant pincer sliced towards him. The pincer bit into the edge of the sturdy wooden shield as if it were made of butter.

"Over here, Sting!" Elenna yelled, distracting the Beast as she drew back her bow and aimed an arrow.

"Leave us, girl," Sting said roughly. "This is not your battle."

"If your battle is with Tom then it's with me," Elenna retorted, releasing her arrow. It hit the Beast's stomach but his skin was like armour, and the arrow bounced off, falling to the ground. Sting roared in annoyance and turned to Elenna.

Tom staggered to his feet, eager to protect his friend, but Silver got there first, racing in to bite at Sting's scaly legs. Storm also cantered forwards and reared up, lashing out at the

Beast with his hooves. Sting snapped his pincers like scissors, slicing at Storm's mane.

Tom felt a surge of pride as he saw his friends bravely fight the Beast. At the same moment, he heard a rattling sound from the tomb. Arcta was struggling against the second silver chain. His strength was returning! Tom gripped his sword tightly; he knew he needed to deal with Sting before he could free the good Beast.

Tom called Storm and Silver away from the scorpion man, while Elenna let loose another arrow. This time it embedded itself in Sting's neck, which was still soft and human. With a screech of pain, Sting flung his hand to the arrow and tried to pull it out. It gave Tom the chance he had been looking for. He raised his sword,

and charged forwards, ready to strike
at Sting's heart.

But Tom wasn't prepared for the
Beast's powerful tail. It flew towards
him like lightning. Tom just managed
to avoid being crushed by its weight,
but the jewel at the tail's tip cut deep
into his cheek.

Tom could feel the warm blood
trickling down his face. He looked up

to see Sting's tail coming towards him again. With a surge of anger he whirled his sword and swung it upwards, slicing the tip of the tail clean off.

Sting screamed, the sound shaking the walls. The tip of his tail flew across the chamber and hit the floor in a spurt of black blood. The purple gem came loose from its setting, rolling across the chamber floor towards Elenna. She bent down and snatched it up, sharing a triumphant glance with Tom. They had the final jewel!

Tom could hear Arcta still struggling to free himself from the second silver chain as Sting turned on Elenna, mad with pain. Tom tried to get past the Beast's injured tail, but even without its tip, it was still powerful and knocked him to his knees every time.

Suddenly there was a crash from the tomb. Tom whirled around.

"Arcta!" he shouted joyfully. "You're free!"

The mountain giant had managed to pull himself away from the second chain. With a roof-shaking roar, he climbed to his feet and pounded on his chest.

The chamber walls trembled and fragments of rock cascaded from the ceiling as Arcta's head brushed the roof. The giant roared again, kicking away one side of his tomb, which fell to the floor with a mighty crash. The foundations of the chamber shuddered, and part of a wall crumbled into a heap. The movement of Arcta's huge bulk was

putting a massive strain on the catacombs. The whole place looked and sounded as if it were about to crash down on top of them!

Sting backed away from Elenna with a snarl, his eyes flickering around the disintegrating chamber before he turned and scuttled down the tunnel towards the trap door.

Arcta bellowed loudly, raising his arms. Tom could feel the good Beast's wild delight at being free. More rocks began to fall to the ground.

"There's no time to lose," Tom called to Elenna. "We have to follow Sting, and get out of these tunnels before everything collapses!"

Narrowly avoiding a shard of rock that speared into the ground beside him, Tom grasped a handful of Storm's mane and pulled himself into the saddle. Elenna jumped up behind him. They began to gallop through the tunnel after Sting. Arcta lumbered after them, with Silver running alongside him.

Straining every muscle, Tom guided Storm between the crashing boulders that fell like giant black hailstones.

Tombs smashed to the ground, spilling their bones into Storm's path. Grimly, Tom pushed on up the steep passageway. In the flickering light, he could see pools of sticky black scorpion blood on the ground. Tom knew that they had to catch Sting before he got to the trap door. He had no doubt that the Beast planned to leave them trapped in the collapsing chamber. Tom reminded himself that Sting had lost a lot of blood and would be getting weaker. There was still time to stop him.

The tunnel began levelling out, and ahead Tom could see Sting scuttling up the great stone steps towards the trap door. With what little strength he had left, the Beast heaved open the hatch and pulled himself out of the hole.

Tom leapt off Storm and sprang forwards.

But he was too late. With a resounding thud, the scorpion man slammed the trap door shut. The torches that lit the catacombs sputtered in the draught, and went out.

Arcta, Tom, Elenna, Storm and Silver were plunged into shaking, rumbling darkness.

CHAPTER TEN

PURPLE MIST

Overhead, Tom could hear Sting ordering guards to hammer Malvel's enchanted bolts into the trap door. The sound of banging started up immediately.

"I'm going to try to push the door open," Tom said, feeling his way up the stairs.

"Good luck," Elenna replied anxiously.

Tom tried with all his might to heave open the trap door. But even with the power of the golden breastplate, it would not budge.

Then Arcta gave a roar and lumbered up the stairs to help. Together, Tom and the mountain giant pushed at the trap door with all their strength.

"Be quick, Tom," Elenna said. "This chamber sounds as if it's going to collapse at any moment."

"It's no good," Tom panted, disappointment flooding through him. "Whatever enchantment Malvel has put on the bolts, it is too strong for Arcta and I."

Tom felt the mountain giant's frustration rush over him like a wave.

"What are we going to do?"

Elenna's voice trembled in the darkness. "There must be another way out."

The ground shook beneath their feet. The shuddering tunnel walls threatened to cave in at any moment. In that instant, Tom wished more than anything that he could be home in Avantia.

Kerlo's words suddenly echoed in his mind. *"Home is like a jewel,"* the gatekeeper had said. *"And it is only once it has gone that you realise how precious it is."* Had the gatekeeper been trying to give him some kind of clue?

"Do you still have Sting's jewel, Elenna?" Tom asked, leaving the stairs and feeling his way along the tunnel towards his friend.

There was a glow of purple light

as Elenna drew the gem from her pocket. Tom took it carefully and held it up in front of him. The light began to pulse. Then Tom felt his hand begin to move through the air, drawing a doorway in the stone wall with the edge of the jewel.

With a rush of delight, Tom realised that the jewel was cutting a magical gateway that would get them out of the catacombs.

Far above them, Tom could hear Malvel's castle groaning and crumbling. The collapsing catacombs must have damaged the very foundations of the castle.

"Stand close to me," Tom commanded, as more rocks fell around them.

His hand was still moving, the jewel drawing the last part of the new gateway. The darkness peeled away in a sharp, clear line. Beyond the freshly cut door, a purple mist swirled and beckoned.

"Tom," Elenna gasped, her eyes shining as she clasped Tom's hand. "Do you think this will take us back home to Avantia?"

"I hope so." Tom hardly dared to believe that they were just a step away from their beloved homeland.

In his mind he called to Arcta, telling the good Beast to follow them through the gateway. Then he seized Storm's bridle, while Elenna grasped Silver's scruff, and together they dived into the cool purple mist.

The air stretched. Tom felt himself spinning. Bright lights glowed all around him.

"Goodbye, Tom and Elenna, goodbye..." Kerlo's voice echoed about them.

Tom started to say thank you to the gatekeeper, but an awful scream, full of fury, interrupted him. It was Malvel.

"You have not seen the last of

me, Tom," Malvel screeched. "I will be victorious!"

But just as the words left Malvel's mouth, the wizard suddenly gave a shriek of fear. Tom could hear the sound of tumbling, crashing rock, and then nothing more.

Tom sensed the massive bulk of Arcta spinning beside him. Then the giant seemed to disappear, and Tom, Elenna, Storm and Silver landed on the familiar floor of King Hugo's throne room, where the King and Wizard Aduro were waiting expectantly for them.

"Welcome home," smiled Aduro, holding out his hands in greeting. "I knew you would prevail, Tom. Congratulations! You have defeated Malvel once again and, although I could not see as clearly as I would have liked, I believe that the Dark Wizard was crushed beneath the rubble of his own castle."

Tom felt a wave of relief surge through him as he embraced Aduro, but this was quickly replaced with panic. Where was Arcta? Had the giant somehow been pulled back into Gorgonia?

"Arcta has returned to his rightful place – in the mountains," said King Hugo, sensing his worry.
He rose from his throne. "Well done, Tom. You are truly Avantia's greatest champion."

Tom bowed his head. While the King thanked Elenna for all her help, Tom looked out of one of the throne-room windows. The sky was sapphire-blue, and the sun shone gently down on the green land that surrounded the castle. Brightly coloured flags and pennants fluttered on the houses in the distance. They had escaped the swirling red fog of evil Gorgonia for ever.

"We are holding a feast in your honour in the Great Hall today," King Hugo announced, as he stroked Storm and Silver in turn. "Avantia is impatient to welcome home her heroes."

A liveried servant walked in and draped a soft woollen blanket over Storm's back, before leading the stallion away for food and a warm stable full of fresh bedding. Tom looked down at the purple jewel that still lay in his hand. He slipped it into his belt. The row of six jewels glowed fiercely, filling the throne room with a rainbow of light and power. The others looked on in wonder.

Then King Hugo clapped an arm around Tom's shoulder, and Aduro walked between Elenna and Silver. Together, they all moved towards the palace stairway and down to the bustle of the Great Hall below, where the feast was being laid out. Brightly suited servants carried groaning trays of food, and musicians tuned their instruments in the minstrels' gallery. The citizens of Avantia were already streaming excitedly through the palace doors in their finest clothes, and the air was buzzing with chatter and laughter.

As Tom took his place at the top table between King Hugo and Elenna, his thoughts strayed to Malvel and Seth, the boy who had turned into a Beast. What had become of them? Had they really perished in the ruins of the castle? Then he thought of Odora and the Gorgonian rebels he had helped to escape into Avantia. Where were they now?

Shaking the thoughts from his head, he turned to Elenna and raised his glass. "Here's to the completion of another Beast Quest," Tom said. "I couldn't have done it without you, Elenna."

Elenna chinked her glass against Tom's and with her other hand fed some chicken to Silver, who sat at her feet. "You're welcome, Tom," she said cheerfully. Then she noticed her friend's serious expression. "But why don't you smile? Malvel has gone at last and it's all down to us!"

Tom drank deeply from his goblet, then grinned at his friend. He would allow himself to smile today – but only time would tell whether they had seen the last of Malvel!

JOIN TOM ON HIS NEXT BEAST QUEST SOON!

Look out for Series 4

THE AMULET
OF AVANTIA

Only Tom can defeat the
Ghost Beasts and save
his father . . .

Look out for

SPIROS
THE GHOST
PHOENIX

Special bumper edition!

CHAPTER ONE

THE EVIL OF MALVEL

"Do you realise where we are, Tom?" said
Elenna, as he helped her over a fallen trunk.
Silver bounded over to stand beside Tom's
stallion, Storm.

Tom peered through the dense trees. It had
been raining and the smell of damp leaves
filled his nostrils. "In a forest?" he joked.

"This is where we first met!" said Elenna.

Tom thought back. He'd been on a mission
to free Ferno the fire dragon from Malvel the
Dark Wizard's evil curse. "It was my first Beast
Quest," he said. "You were hunting rabbits
with Silver."

"That's right," said Elenna, stroking Silver's
neck. "The forest doesn't seem as frightening
now."

Tom nodded. After all the Beasts they'd faced
together, the darkness of the forest no longer
made him shiver. He placed his foot in Storm's
stirrup and heaved himself up. Elenna climbed
into the saddle behind him.

"Once we clear the forest and cross the plains, it's only a short ride to Errinel," said Elenna.

Tom smiled. "I can't wait. It's been so long since I last saw my aunt and uncle. Something to eat and a soft bed is just what we need after all our adventures."

Silver barked and jumped up on his hind legs.

"And there might even be some bones for you!" laughed Elenna.

Tom steered his stallion across the mossy forest floor. But something was bothering him. He sensed that he and his friends were not alone. He let his hand drop onto the hilt of his sword.

"What's wrong?" Elenna asked.

A sound like a crack of lightning splintered the silence, and a cloud of smoke appeared between the trees. Tom slipped from the saddle, unsheathing his sword and gripping his shield. Silver whimpered and Storm swished his tail.

"Is it Malvel?" whispered Elenna, dismounting.

But as the smoke cleared, a familiar figure

emerged. He was wearing a cloak of faded blue and red silk.

"Aduro!" said Elenna, rushing forwards.

Tom put away his sword. But the look in the old man's grey eyes made him anxious. "What is it, Aduro?" he asked.

"I had to come immediately," said the good wizard.

Even Silver stopped leaping about, and Elenna fell back beside Tom.

Aduro stroked his wispy beard. "Tom, Elenna, you must steel yourselves for terrible news," he warned. "Malvel has committed his worst crime yet."

Fear crept over Tom's heart. He felt Elenna's fingers grip his arm.

Aduro looked Tom in the eye. "A messenger arrived at King Hugo's castle this morning with a dreadful tale. Last night a weary traveller came to your village. The local tavern owner thought there was something unusual about him, but your Uncle Henry and Aunt Maria, kind people that they are, gave him a meal and a bed for the night. This morning they were gone. And so was the traveller."

"Perhaps they offered to accompany him to his destination," said Tom.

"I'm afraid not," said Aduro. "The traveller left behind a message…" The wizard pulled out a piece of parchment from his cloak and handed it to Tom.

He unfolded the thin paper and read: "'Dear Tom, if I cannot hurt you, I will kill those closest to you. Malvel.'"

"Oh, Tom!" gasped Elenna.

Tom felt sick. His hand clenched into a fist around the parchment.
"I'll rescue Uncle Henry and Aunt Maria," he vowed. "While there's blood in my veins, I won't rest until I get them back."

Follow this Quest to the end in SPIROS THE GHOST PHOENIX.

Win an exclusive
Beast Quest T-shirt and goody bag!

In every Beast Quest book the Beast Quest logo is hidden
in one of the pictures. Find the logos in book 13 to book
18 and make a note of which pages they appear on.
Send the six page numbers to us. Each month we will
draw one winner to receive a Beast Quest T-shirt
and goody bag.

Send your entry on a postcard listing
the title of this book and the winning
page number to:

THE BEAST QUEST COMPETITION:
STING THE SCORPION MAN
Orchard Books
338 Euston Road, London NW1 3BH
Australian readers should email:
childrens.books@hachette.com.au

New Zealand readers should write to:
Beast Quest Competition
4 Whetu Place, Mairangi Bay, Auckland, NZ
or email: childrensbooks@hachette.co.nz

Only one entry per child.
Final draw: 31 October 2009

You can also enter this competition
via the Beast Quest website: www.beastquest.co.uk

Fight the Beasts,
Fear the Magic

www.beastquest.co.uk

Have you checked out the all-new Beast Quest website?
It's the place to go for games, downloads, activities,
sneak previews and lots of fun!

You can read all about your favourite Beast Quest
monsters, download free screensavers and desktop
wallpapers for your computer, and send
beastly e-cards to your friends.

Sign up to the newsletter at www.beastquest.co.uk
to receive exclusive extra content and the opportunity
to enter special members-only competitions. It's the best
place to go for up-to-date info on all the Beast Quest
books, including the next exciting series,
which features six brand new Beasts.

Series 1

Ferno the Fire Dragon	978 1 84616 483 5
Sepron the Sea Serpent	978 1 84616 482 8
Arcta the Mountain Giant	978 1 84616 484 2
Tagus the Horse-Man	978 1 84616 486 6
Nanook the Snow Monster	978 1 84616 485 9
Epos the Flame Bird	978 1 84616 487 3

Vedra & Krimon: Twin Beasts of Avantia	978 1 84616 951 9

Series 2: The Golden Armour

Zepha the Monster Squid	978 1 84616 988 5
Claw the Giant Monkey	978 1 84616 989 2
Soltra the Stone Charmer	978 1 84616 990 8
Vipero the Snake Man	978 1 84616 991 5
Arachnid the King of Spiders	978 1 84616 992 2
Trillion the Three-Headed Lion	978 1 84616 993 9

Spiros the Ghost Phoenix	978 1 84616 994 6

Series 3: The Dark Realm

Torgor the Minotaur	978 1 84616 997 7
Skor the Winged Stallion	978 1 84616 998 4
Narga the Sea Monster	978 1 40830 000 8
Kaymon the Gorgon Hound	978 1 40830 001 5
Tusk the Mighty Mammoth	978 1 40830 002 2
Sting the Scorpion Man	978 1 40830 003 9

All priced at £4.99
Vedra & Krimon: Twin Beasts of Avantia and *Spiros the Ghost Phoenix* are priced at £5.99

The Beast Quest books are available from all good
bookshops, or can be ordered direct from the publisher:
Orchard Books, PO BOX 29, Douglas IM99 1BQ.
Credit card orders please telephone 01624 836000
or fax 01624 837033 or visit our website: www.orchardbooks.co.uk
or e-mail: bookshop@enterprise.net for details.

To order please quote title, author
and ISBN and your full name and address.
Cheques and postal orders should be made payable to 'Bookpost plc.'
Postage and packing is FREE within the UK
(overseas customers should add £2.00 per book).

Prices and availability are subject to change.